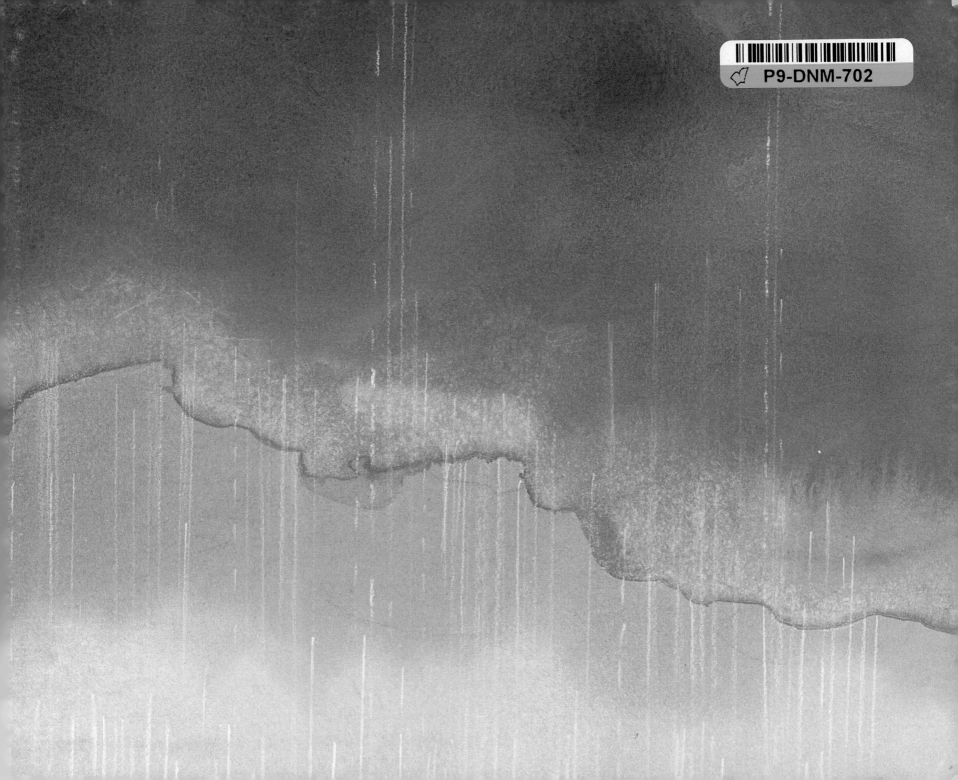

To everyone who forgot
their umbrella today.
I love you, Bee.

*amy June*

To all my friends, especially the pink,
speckled, many-legged ones.
I love you too, Mom.

*Juniper*

SIMON & SCHUSTER
BOOKS FOR YOUNG READERS
An imprint of Simon & Schuster Children's Publishing Division
1230 Avenue of the Americas, New York, New York 10020
Copyright © 2018 by Amy June Bates

For information about special discounts for bulk purchases, please contact
Simon & Schuster Special Sales at 1-866-506-1949 or business@simonandschuster.com.
The Simon & Schuster Speakers Bureau can bring authors to your live event.
For more information or to book an event, contact the Simon & Schuster Speakers Bureau at 1-866-248-3049
or visit our website at www.simonspeakers.com.
Book design by Laurent Linn • The text for this book was set in pencilPete. • The illustrations for this book were rendered in
watercolor, gouache, and pencil on watercolor paper. • Manufactured in China • 1117 SCP • First Edition • 10 9 8 7 6 5 4 3 2 1
Library of Congress Cataloging-in-Publication Data • Names: Bates, Amy June, author, illustrator. | Bates, Juniper, author.
Title: The big umbrella / Amy June Bates ; cowritten with Juniper Bates.
Description: First Edition. | New York : Schuster Books for Young Readers, [2018] | A Paula Wiseman Book. |
Summary: A spacious umbrella welcomes anyone and everyone who needs shelter from the rain.
Identifiers: LCCN 2017015622| ISBN 9781534406582 (hardback) | ISBN 9781534406599 (e-book)
Subjects: | CYAC: Toleration—Fiction. | Emigration and immigration—Fiction. | Umbrellas—Fiction. | BISAC: JUVENILE FICTION / Social Issues / Values & Virtues. |
JUVENILE FICTION / Social Issues / Emigration & Immigration. | JUVENILE FICTION / Social Issues / Prejudice & Racism.
Classification: LCC PZ7.B29444146 Bi 2018 | DDC [E]—dc23 LC record available at https://lccn.loc.gov/2017015622

# THE
# BIG
# UMBRELLA

## Amy June Bates
### Cowritten with Juniper Bates

A Paula Wiseman Book
SIMON & SCHUSTER
BOOKS FOR YOUNG READERS
New York   London   Toronto   Sydney   New Delhi

By the front door . . .

there is an umbrella.

It is big.

It is a **big, friendly** umbrella.

It likes to help.

It likes to
spread its arms wide.

It loves to

give shelter.

It loves to
gather people in.

It doesn't matter

if you are tall

or hairy

or plaid.

It doesn't matter
how many legs you have.

Some people worry that there won't be enough room under the big umbrella.

But the amazing thing is . . .

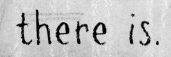

there is.

There is always room.